PRIDE

Jane Austen

List of Characters

Miss Elizabeth Bennet

Mr Darcy

Miss Jane Bennet

Miss Lydia Bennet

Mr Bingley

Mr Wickham

Mrs Bennet

Mr Bennet

Pride and Prejudice

In 30 seconds:

The romance of Elizabeth Bennet and Mr Darcy has delighted readers ever since *Pride and Prejudice* was first published in 1813. Before the couple can be happy, Elizabeth must overcome her pride at hearing Mr Darcy's insult on their first meeting, and Mr Darcy must conquer his prejudice against Elizabeth's inferior social standing. Jane Austen's world-famous novel shows that courtship in the late eighteenth and early nineteenth centuries was influenced by strict ideas of reputation and class, but proves that true love can triumph over these obstacles.

In five words:

Love, courtship, reputation, class, society

Other novels by Jane Austen:

Sense and Sensibility, Mansfield Park, Emma, Northanger Abbey, Persuasion

Not all of the characters in the novel *Pride and Prejudice* are illustrated on this concertina. Read the novel to discover Mr Collins, who also proposes to Elizabeth, and Mr Darcy's rich aunt, Catherine de Bourgh.

First published in 2015 by Frances Lincoln Children's Books,
74-77 White Lion Street, London N1 9PF
This edition published by Rock Point a division of
Quarto Publishing Group USA Inc.
276 Fifth Avenue, Suite 206
New York, New York 10001
Pride and Prejudice Unfolded © Frances Lincoln Limited 2015
Illustrations © Becca Stadtlander 2015
All rights reserved. ISBN: 978-1-63106-141-7
Printed in China.
1 3 5 7 9 10 8 6 4 2

"'It is settled between us already, that we are to be the happiest couple in the world.'"

To Mrs Bennet's delight, Mr Darcy and Elizabeth, and Mr Bingley and Jane, are married.

'It is a truth universally acknowledged, that a single man in possession of a good fortune, must be in want of a wife.'

The arrival of Mr Bingley and Mr Darcy at Netherfield is discussed by the Bennets.

"'She is tolerable, but not handsome
enough to tempt me; I am in no humour at present
to give consequence to young ladies who are
slighted by other men.'"

At a ball, Mr Bingley and Jane dance twice.
Elizabeth overhears Mr Darcy being rude about her...

"'You are too generous to trifle with me. If your feelings are still what they were last April, tell me so at once.'"

Darcy tells Elizabeth that his feelings for her are unchanged. She accepts his marriage proposal.

"Oh! Lizzy, why am I thus singled from my family, and blessed above them all! If I could but see you as happy! If there were but such another man for you!"

Mr Bingley returns to the Bennet residence and proposes to Jane, who he has loved from the beginning.

"'I have been meditating on the very great pleasure which a pair of fine eyes in the face of a pretty woman can bestow.'"

But during the next weeks, Darcy begins to look on Elizabeth more favorably.

"The whole party have left Netherfield by this time, and are on their way to town—and without any intention of coming back again."

Jane is parted from Mr Bingley as he is persuaded to leave Netherfield by Mr Darcy.

'He had done all this for a girl whom he could neither regard nor esteem. Her heart did whisper that he had done it for her. But it was a hope shortly checked by other considerations...'

Elizabeth learns from her aunt that it was Mr Darcy that bribed Wickham to marry Lydia, saving her sister's reputation.

"'Well, mamma... and what do you think of my husband? Is not he a charming man? I am sure my sisters must all envy me.'"

Wickham is somehow persuaded to marry Lydia, and the newlyweds return to the Bennet family home.

'"The late Mr Darcy meant to provide for me amply, and thought he had done it; but when the living fell, it was given elsewhere."'

The militia arrive, and Elizabeth is told by Mr Wickham how Mr Darcy cruelly cheated him out of his inheritance.

"'In vain I have struggled. It will not do. My feelings will not be repressed. You must allow me to tell you how ardently I admire and love you.'"

Mr Darcy proposes to Elizabeth. Upset by his first opinion of her, and his actions towards Jane and Mr Wickham, she refuses.

"They are gone off together from Brighton. You know him too well to doubt the rest. She has no money, no connections, nothing that can tempt him to—she is lost forever."

Elizabeth learns that Mr Wickham has seduced her younger sister, Lydia, potentially ruining her family's standing in society.

'Never in her life had she seen his manners so little dignified, never had he spoken with such gentleness as on this unexpected meeting.'

Elizabeth visits Pemberley, Mr Darcy's estate, where she sees Mr Darcy again. She realizes her feelings for him are changing.

'Georgiana was persuaded to believe herself in love, and to consent to an elopement. She was then but fifteen, which must be her excuse...'

Elizabeth learns the truth: that Mr Wickham gambled away his inheritance and seduced Darcy's younger sister for her money.